A SCHOOL FOR

POMPEY WALKER

A SCHOOL FOR

By Michael J. Rosen

Illustrated by Aminah Brenda Lynn Robinson

POMPEY WALKER

Harcourt Brace & Company

San Diego   New York   London

Printed in Singapore

Now, enough of that—I don't deserve such fussing. Applauding for Pompey Walker! Who would have thought anybody'd applaud a man who spent so much of his life a slave, and so much more of it a criminal—at least to some eyes. Please. Stop your clapping. I was already next to tears just hearing all your singing of "Lift Every Voice," such a beautiful hymn in this brand-new building—I was already embarrassed (ashamed, almost!) hearing your principal Mrs. Gilbert's too-nice words about me and the single good thing I did so long ago I hardly think it was me that did it. Just give me a second to ready this story of a slave, name of Pompey, who, by the grace of God and one of His good men, stole his life again and again from the evil that was the whole of slavery.

You see, simply being inside a school, where there's learning to be had, means being in a place that for my childhood and well into my adulthood was ever and only a dream.

Promise me, first, you won't look to an almost-ninety-year-old man for a real speaker's kind of speech. Truthfully, I don't feel all that real at ninety. This name that I am leaving behind here at this school will belong to each of you maybe even more than it ever honestly belonged to me.

—No, Mrs. Gilbert, I do not know the name my mother gave me back in eighteen-and-thirty-five. Must be there, buried somewhere on that Georgia plantation where she lived and probably died. Name the planter called me was Pompey. Lots of slaves there had classical-sounding names; I myself knew a Caesar, an Augustus, a Caius—even a Zeus. Makes us slaves sound like important leaders and rulers, doesn't it?

As for my last name, it was the same as every other piece of property—person, animal, thing, or building—on that hellful place, and it was Bibb.

But you children didn't ask this old man to speak at this dedicating of your school just to watch him try and recall what he can't remember. No, you didn't. So close your eyes, maybe, and see if you can picture me when I was the age of the very youngest of you here—at least to start my telling. Will you forgive me if I can't tell my story like a good book? Maybe afterward, teachers, you can read these children a good story.

Now, what can I remember? Hmm—what's more like it is: What haven't I been able to forget. . . .

Pompey's tale begins with crows. Earliest thing I can recall is my mother—name of Eulalie Bibb—and I'm feeding at her breast while she is working cotton fields. This is all the world she or I know, the fields of a planter named Mr. Charles Bibb. I'm three years old, most probably—I haven't started my own picking-cotton work. Whenever the sun is anywhere in the sky, my old mother is working the fields, and I am waiting in the hundred-degree shade of a willow. Who are my playmates? Big black-as-coal crows, big as I am. No, they don't sing lullabies like birdies in some picture books—are no picture books or any other kind for a slave child. No, they don't eat seed corn right from my hands—*is* no extra corn for them or for us. Crows are just living their coming-and-going lives nearby and beside me.

See, I'll tell you about the crows and maybe spare this room full up of innocent children, who will never suffer such things, some of what all I know of the foulest and most cruel piece of time that ate up and spit out forty million people from most of Africa and the Indies. Know how I know that number? Learned it in a book that I myself read. You are so blessed, each and every one of you. Learning and books are yours every day. First book my eyes knew what to do with, I was twenty-two years of age. Before that, my only book was the one I made with my two open hands put together like this. Only thing in that book would be the tears I cried, plenty of evenings. I could recite the ways and shapes of misery from A to Z, though I didn't know a single letter back then. You see, a slave who could read was a dangerous, instigating, wily threat of a . . . Negro. That's the lie I heard every day, more often than grace. Now, I'm going to use that right and politest word "Negro," not that I ever heard anything as respecting as that at the time—no, then it was only hate-filled names for people with black skin—I just hope I don't get caught up in the retelling and use the words most natural to those hideous times.

So those crows fly through all my first years. After my mother's milk, there is only pork fat and hoecakes to eat. *Hoecakes?* You mix cornmeal with water and pile it on the hoe—the one you use for your little garden (sometimes we're allowed a little garden). And you cook that over hot coals just to browning. This is what I eat, what all the slaves on the Bibb place eat, day after day. Once in a while, there's molasses, or a melon someone steals, and liquor. Yes, I have to confess I am drinking pitifully with all the children.

There's a saying about eating I hear sometimes when we meet in the earliest morning, way before light, for a secret prayer meeting. (No Bibb slaves can meet together: not for praying, not for anything, on account of meetings make slaves want to escape. That's another thing they tell us.) The man who knows the most about preaching, he says to us sometimes, "Slaves plant the corn. Hogs eat the corn. Slaves eat the hogs. Masters eat the slaves." 'Course he uses that more vicious word for slaves.

After crows come horses. Long stables filled with the handsomest of God's creations, and that's where my adult work begins— I am all of seven years, maybe, and that's adult enough to work. I keep on saying "maybe" because I don't know my birthday. It's just some time around the planting time for cotton seeds. If I did know the exact day, wouldn't do me any good—I can't read a calendar; plus, no one here, except probably the people in the main house, has a calendar. A slave day is all the daylight hours for

working, and whatever's left for cooking and carrying on life with as little sleep as possible. And a slave year? Weeks and months may pass, but how we tell time's passing is by the planting seasons and when the hottest weather comes and goes and the lasting of sicknesses you get and the span it takes for a foal to quit its nursing and when the new clothes are given out and by seeing how other children get tall and how old people, more and more of them, get weaker.

With all the horses comes Jeremiah Walker. He is married to one of the planter's daughters, Mary Catherine Bibb Walker. Jeremiah comes all the time to ride his horse, Starbright, but so far, I don't know this white man to speak to him. Still, this is where the seed of my freedom is sowed. If I could name that day, that day would be a better birthday for me, the sowing of that seed of freedom.

Picture me a boy shoveling straw and manure and carrying buckets of water. (Ignore this old, wrinkled face.) I'm growing up some, doing these chores, caring for the master's stable. A child should be learning, right? And I *am* learning—not much for my brain, but plenty of learning for my hands and my back. I've learned everything about horses: grooming, shoeing, plus how it feels to be kicked by, and stepped on by, and bit by a horse, and how a horse rolls over sick to death with colic . . . everything except about riding a horse. Never that. No slave boy ever gets to ride a horse, though I do ride when my eyes close around midnight. Those sleeping rides no one can stop even with a horsewhip, which

I see used on men's naked backs more than on any of these prize horses.

I work those stables, and when I'm done working them, I sleep in them, never seeing my family (meaning only my mother), except maybe on Saturday and most of Sunday. Point of fact: The hayloft is lots softer than the dirt which is the bed my mother has, the bed all the other Bibbs who work those cotton fields have to share. *Cotton fields,* hear me—they're sleeping on dirt while their all-day, back-breaking work is making the softest thing God created to sleep on.

A story shouldn't be longer than a life, so I'll hurry. I said the name Jeremiah Walker, and you know standing before you is one Pompey Walker. This particular day that Jeremiah comes to ride, I am Pompey Bibb, a school-age boy without a school. He is a man of eighteen or so. I'm twelve and awfully big for my age—tall, all legs, and skinny. All of us slaves, except the house slaves, are skinny. Clothes don't fit me—never have, since there's but two shirts and two pants a year that I don't know if I'll wear out or grow out of first. No socks, nothing underneath. So imagine me this one day with the planter's folks inside the stables. There's Jeremiah on his horse with his father-in-law the planter, and more of the Bibb people nearby. Then all of a sudden, that abiding and gentle mare, Starbright, rears up for no reason anyone can see and hurls Jeremiah across the fence and down to the ground. Jeremiah's leg is twisted so queerly beside him, looks like it belongs to someone else entirely. So everyone rushes to Jeremiah, and I rush to do what I figure my job is: to lead Starbright back in her stall.

Soon as I'm back, Mr. Charles Bibb tells his slave-driver, Abraham—a soulless man my own color—he tells him, "Tie that boy's hands to the corral," and tells him to whip me I-don't-know-how-many times, since the pain has me fainting long before he's finished. No, a horse's rearing like that could never have been a white man's fault. Never could have been the horse's fault, neither. Or the hornet's fault for stinging Starbright on the lip—I saw the stinging sore later; I'd even told them about the hornets' nest the week before, right over the barn door, and nobody did a thing about that, either. No, that accident was the fault of the lazy stable boy who somehow didn't do the horse right. So this day it's Pompey the stable boy's fault, even though Jeremiah is yelling *no no no,* at least as long as I'm conscious and hearing, to his father and to Abraham, that slave-driver whipping a boy but twelve years old.

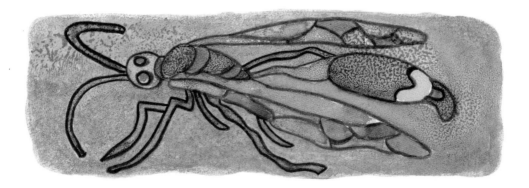

Some of you bigger boys must be about that, right? Thank the Lord, a torturing like that will never touch your precious skins. That was my first, though no one can make me count up how many whippings more brought me here to this place.

Horses are all my kith and kin for another and another year, and I'm grateful for their company, though Jeremiah comes to be the nearest to a friend a slave can have. Understand, that doesn't mean more than a few kind words and occasional times when I am asked for a reply. He's usually with his other people and they often say to him, "Why you being so nice to that Negro boy?" But every day he rides Starbright he thanks me for treating his horse with the kind of love that a person has for something that's his own. But *owning?* I don't own a thing except what I can remember . . . and I'd have given away nearly most of those memories if I could have.

Jeremiah's wife is a truly beautiful woman, an educated teacher, and she is schooling all her sisters' and brothers' children. A one-room schoolhouse sits right on the property. Sometimes she has her lessons in the peach orchard right alongside the stables. She reads aloud a lot to her nieces and nephews. The horses are usually quiet and I can hear her voice. Sometimes she reads extra loud if she sees me around. Kind—she is kind as Jeremiah, but still, all the planter's grandchildren are there, and the smallest word from any one of them about a loafing slave boy will have me whipped or worse.

That overhearing is my first school; lasts me nearly a year. It remains my lone schooling for many more years. Sometimes, while I'm working, I try to say aloud the words she is teaching that day, memorizing parts of poems; I get the sound of those rhyming words all right, but only once in a while, a little of what they mean.

Then the saddest thing happens. That teacher, Mrs. Jeremiah Walker, she dies, taking with her most of Jeremiah's happiness and my only schooling, too. She dies giving birth to their first child and that nameless child dies right with her. I don't see that, of course, but I have seen infants dying in the cotton fields from the heat or from what-all I can't say. There's a graveyard—some lined-up stones is all—back of the slave quarters: slaves and children dead before slaving could kill them.

Times are terrible for Negroes, but still they don't shower luck every day on the white folks. When he comes riding, I can see Jeremiah's sadness. I see it when he rides Starbright like a man who's lost everything, which isn't true because he still has that wondrous horse, still has a partial right, sooner or later, to his father-in-law's acres, and still has his being white, which is a gift and a fortune no slave, however hard he works, is ever going to earn. And that's not saying a single slave I ever knew wanted to be white—no, we just wanted the privileges that came with it and didn't cost a thing, let alone a person's life.

Told you about the crows, I did, and the horses and Jeremiah, so I can't go any further without telling something of the dogs. Except for flies, isn't anything more everywhere than dogs on that plantation. Mr. Charles Bibb has mastiffs—giant, big-headed dogs larger than any of you here. He breeds enough of these dogs to terrorize the entire South. And every one of them is mean. You'd guess maybe he starves them all, like he does the slaves, to make them that mean, but no, no, they eat pounds of fresh meat every day. Meanest mastiff of all is the one Abraham's got; that slave-driver could turn the gentlest rabbit mean.

Everywhere else, there are gentle dogs: mongrels and mutts nobody owns that just live nearby us slaves—not that we have

anything to give them but our singing and, honest to God, the tears in our eyes, which they like to lick. For the salt, I guess.

One dog I name Cinders. She shows up one day at the stables and pretty much stays with me until her last. Sleeps beside me, except on those airless, hottest nights when the only thing that moves the air is mosquito wings. If a boy can have a friend that isn't another boy or any human being whatsoever, then Cinders is who I have.

Day before what turns out to be my last day on Mr. Charles Bibb's plantation, Cinders gives birth to seven puppies. Right there in among the bales of hay in the stables. I know, without a soul telling me, to hide that litter anywhere I can. So I stay up with the noise of the barn owls and the bats, just witnessing those puppies come into the world. Right after she licks them all clean and has them nursing, Abraham comes in with his mastiff. They look over at Cinders and her newborns and he says, "Mr. Bibb don't want more of your slave dogs here," and without a second thought, he turns loose that devil-dog of his.

Before I can even stand, his giant dog has Cinders in his jaws, shaking her like something sticky he can't get off. When I'm finally able to jerk that mad dog's back legs out from under him, I start swinging him around—only way not to get bit. Abraham doesn't dare take out his whip, since he'd likely strike his own dog. The Lord's the only one who knows how I have the strength to spin that beast. Finally, Abraham grabs his dog, leashes him again, and tells me, just like nothing's dying right there and then, "I was heading down to pick a few of you worthless troublemakers to sell tomorrow. Georgia-trader's in town. You, you're going to be gone by daybreak." *Georgia-trader*—that's a slave-dealer, plain and simple.

But before I'm delivered into those ruthless hands, between sunrise and this very despairing moment I'm up to in my telling, I sit by that wounded mother dog with her just-newborn pups nursing on her; they're probably getting as much blood as milk. I don't have the knowing and maybe not even the courage to help Cinders, though her pups are drinking their first milk entirely unaware that it's all their mother will ever have for them. When the sky starts to brighten—picture me now—I'm crying like the baby I still am, and I take up each of those now-motherless puppies and give them each the only blessing I have—which is Godspeed, quickening their starving journey on Earth. And I manage to bury them, too, before Abraham comes back for me.

Give me one second here, so my eyes'll stop this and give me back a voice.

I won't be insulted—say it: "What's that fool of an old man doing with tears from seventy-five years ago?" Maybe your teachers can explain that later. Seems like I got some unused-up tears for whatever struck-down life I ever did cry over in my days. Must all be stored up inside somewhere, since each retelling squeezes out a few old tears.

There, I've tucked my handkerchief away, and I'll go on.

What's next are years of another kind of animal I meet again and again: it's another breed of mankind: man-*un*kind—a beastly, slave-driving, slave-chasing, slave-beating creature. So now I find myself in handcuffs and footcuffs, standing in a linked-up line of slaves—we are a gigantic, God-size necklace, though no God could have worn his creations in such a bondage. Before the auction begins, the looking-to-buy owners arrive to inspect our bodies and our faces, which we've had to wash and oil so we'll look healthy, which not a single one of us is. But I am maybe the healthiest; I'm one of the youngest in the line of men—maybe even the luckiest, since I've lived but one place until that moment.

I hear it: the screaming of children no older than you young-gest ones; they're being sold forever from their mothers. And the heartbreaking shouts of husbands dragged from their once-wives. Planters don't honor a marriage of slaves, don't care one bit about a slave family's rightful ties to one another. My own mother, Eulalie Bibb herself, doesn't know I am gone from her world—then and for all time. Standing in that line of slaves, I rightly figure that no one knows or cares where Bibb's young stable boy up and went.

When it's my turn to be sold, the auctioneer shows everyone my teeth, lifts my eyelids, tells me jump up and down, pulls aside my shirt to let the whipping scars reveal what kind of troublesome slave I might be. "Can you read, boy?" they ask. "No," I say, and I think for the shortest second that maybe whoever buys me will teach me that reading. "Have you ever escaped?" they ask. I say no to that, too, though I have heard stories of slaves sneaking off at night and running away; no one knows what happens after that . . . freedom? All's we hear about are the ones that fail.

So the bidding starts among several men, and finally, from the very back—all's I hear is a voice—a man says eight hundred dollars and the auctioneer says sold and it's over. Pompey's sold—to whom, I don't know. For what work, I don't know. Can you guess anything I'm feeling? A boy just in his first teens, pulled from the only world he knows, even if it wasn't a joyful world at all, and handed over to a stranger for whatever use he can put a human body to.

Who is my new master? No one else but Jeremiah Walker.

Jeremiah Walker, son-in-law of Charles Bibb. He had heard whatever lies Abraham told of my attacking his dog. And he tells me he's stood by and watched all he can stand of the goings-on at that brutalizing plantation. He's finished with that Godless place, he says—his wife is gone and, maybe, at long last, so's most of Jeremiah's grieving for her. "I came to this auction to buy a slave," he tells me, "to set him free in this world, a free man."

Children, that free man was supposed to be me. Now, have you been taught how there was no being free for any Negro, man or woman, at that time, in that South? Any white person at all could stop you, question you, take you for an escaped slave, beat you or jail you or whatever else his devil prompted him to do. And I'm little more than a boy who doesn't know beyond his own first name and some things

about caring for horses. And if there is some way, or some people, like an Underground Railroad to hide and smuggle and deliver runaway slaves to freedom, well, I don't know where such a railroad station is supposed to be—and that's the ignorance I suffer under every day like it's a beating-down hot sun.

So I say, "Jeremiah Walker, even if you possess the kindness to grant me my freedom, how am I supposed to accept it here?" The most powerful wish I have is to be gone from that place forever; but without money, without a horse, without clothes, with nothing to tell me which way is true freedom and real schooling and a proud life for an honest man—with nothing but the North Star— there is no place my granted freedom can take me but back to someone else's slavery. (Should I be embarrassed to tell you children this? . . . I don't know, but the boy I am at the telling of this story can't even name you two free states where a Negro can try for a peaceful life.)

I'm not so much afraid at this moment as I am simply unknowing of how this news of Jeremiah's can be lived out. *Lived,* I say, because I'm plenty knowing of how that news can bring me closer to dead.

So Jeremiah says to me, "Abraham brought you here without my even knowing it. I didn't call you my own, but you worked closer to me than to anyone. So now I have paid my own father-in-law for you, and you are done slaving for him, and you're not going to work for me, Pompey. A free man is what you are."

Before I can even put my thoughts in a question, two men on horseback ride over to us; two tied-up slaves are slung over the back of a third horse like feed sacks.

"Hey, Mr. Walker," they call to Jeremiah. We're standing beside the pen where the horses and hogs still to be auctioned are. We're minding our own business. "I do believe we just found us two of Mr. Bibb's runaway slaves. Recognize these worthless fellows?"

Jeremiah looks quick at the faces of the slaves—all's anyone's going to recognize is that both men are next-to-dead—and says they most certainly are not from that plantation. It's true we Bibb slaves didn't have a red-hot iron brand on our arms or backs like some slaves did, but the more I look, I think maybe those two tied-up men might have worked alongside my mother.

Then the second white man says, "We got word there's a whole uprising of runaways just heading out, but they won't get across a county, let alone a state line, with all the riders we got recruited."

That's what does it. That stops Jeremiah thinking in his own kind of ignorant way that I'm just going to hop that fence and start walking north with his looking-the-other-way kindness in my pocket as my only protection. And after another moment, he announces something that comes to mean the rest of both of our lives: "My parents live up near Cincinnati. If you're willing enough, join me, as I'm going to Ohio. People there will honor your freedom; they'll know who can help."

Do you think I'm a fool for not trusting, right then and there, this man who looked enough like one slave's earthly savior and truest friend? Well, this much is true: There was no one else I trusted more than Jeremiah Walker. But how far was that trust going to take me?

—Go on, ask . . .

If Jeremiah were here, he'd best answer that, but I'll try on his behalf. Why?—because his wife and child were dead, as I told you. And why else? He could hardly tolerate Mr. Bibb, I came to learn. Nowadays, you'd call him an Abolitionist, I suppose, but then, *he was just doing his living against the practicing of slavery. He'd only come south on account of his wife's kin. And he hadn't seen his own folks in plenty of years. . . . Still, leaving the state of Georgia in the year eighteen-and-forty-nine with a fourteen-year-old slave boy: This was likely a dangerous thing for him. Danger was more than plain old likely for me.*

Next thing, let's see, Jeremiah mounts Starbright, and he pulls me up in front of him. I grab two fistfuls of Starbright's mane and suddenly we're two people on that one beautiful horse. If you're guessing that this is the first time I myself am sitting on a horse's back, you're guessing right. But even though I'm a boy with no experience at riding I also have no fear—at least, no horse-fear compared to the fears I have right then about everything that surely lies ahead in a world where loving-kindness seems to play no part at all.

No sooner does the sun set on that first day than our ride is held up and halted by two white men with guns. Before we stop,

Jeremiah pulls out a pistol of his own and sticks it in my back, where my heart is beating faster than Starbright's panting. "That your slave boy?" they ask of Jeremiah, and he tells these two paddyrollers with nothing but some slave's reward in their hearts, he tells them, "A runaway—tracked him myself. I'll have him back to our plantation by dark."

That lie of Jeremiah's did work—and it would work, from time to time. (Paddyrollers didn't waste time on a slave whose reward someone else is already getting.)

But this first time, being stopped like this, why, it brings to Jeremiah's mind the worry I know we both ought to be feeling. What he does next does no harm, no permanent damage, I can assure you, but it shocks me deep and in a lasting way: He slides off Starbright, takes out his knife, and walks to the tail of the very horse he loves I guess more than he does most people, and commences to cut off half the strands of that long black tail.

Next day, it's me, Pompey the free man, mind you, riding in front of Jeremiah with those horse hairs wrapped around my head like a wig; it's me with my body wrapped in a wool blanket like some chilled sick woman in the feverish heat. Same for the next day and the next, until five paddyrollers on horses stop us, refusing to believe my disguise or what lies Jeremiah Walker tells them of this slave girl he is delivering. "Looks just like a runaway *we're* looking for," they tell him as they surround us. One of them grabs my legs and slides me sideways to the ground, exposing me for the boy I most obviously am.

What happens next is I run like I'm on fire, straight away from there—but what am I thinking? Do I think my freedom is just beyond some finish line and I can just race those last few yards to cross it? Pompey's fast, but not horse-fast. And what Jeremiah can do to stop them, the five of them, the one of him does do. But two men quickly pin his arms behind his back, while the three who have caught me tie my hands and then my legs to a shagbark hickory, and take to whipping me until my shirt and then my skin is striped and cracked like the very shagbark hickory bark. "Now you'll have no problem with that *girl* of yours," they call to Jeremiah, as if he is likely to thank them for their trouble.

Riding—riding? Now, that's impossible for me the next several days—not even slung over Starbright's back like those tied-up slaves we saw come in at the auction. I'm delirious, hardly awake at all; without saying it, we both realize we'll never make it a mile more with me riding Starbright with Jeremiah. Too suspicious, a white man and a black man sharing one horse. So I hide under some dead branches in the brush, and Jeremiah takes however much money he has left and goes to look for whatever kinds of hope it will buy. Then hours or maybe days pass . . . I don't know much more until Jeremiah wakes me again to show me our best chance at salvation: a buggy-wagon, another gun (the paddyrollers took his), some lumber, and a few supplies.

So we set to building a hiding place beneath the floor of this buggy-wagon—it has something like a trapdoor, and it's, oh, maybe only about this deep . . . eighteen inches or so, just deep enough for me to lie curled up like a baby. (Didn't know it then, but I guess we had made our own small "train-car" on that great Underground Railroad.) So we start our ride north again, north and north for days, even though another thing we don't say to each other is how there isn't money enough to take us as north as we need to go.

We pull into a town in South Carolina where an auction is getting readied—dozens of the most wasted-looking slaves I've ever seen . . . some planters looking to make their good profit, other planters looking to buy a minding slave. That's when the one divine-sent idea of my life comes to me and brings with it all the future luck that brought me here to build a school.

"Jeremiah Walker," I say to him, "take me to that auction block. I'm an able-enough body, likely to fetch a decent price. Sell me for all the money we can get." 'Course, he starts refusing me before I even finish, but I insist he hear me out. "Sell me, collect that money, find out who has bought me and where I'm headed, and then follow soon as you can. I'll escape, somehow. Tonight or tomorrow or the next day. And you find me before the bloodhounds do."

Oh, those bloodhounds . . . that's another kind of dog I came to know, but blessedly, from a distance. All the while we are riding Jeremiah points out signs that I can see plain as day but can't know the meaning of. And he reads me the words. Signs everywhere, advertising: BLOODHOUNDS! MAGNIFICENT PACK OF HOUNDS FOR TRAILING AND CATCHING RUNAWAY SLAVES. Every word I see makes me ache for reading, if only so I can know what-all words mean me harm and what others don't.

Jeremiah Walker takes my idea. It's the only suggestion we've got. Turns out that selling me brings nine hundred and fifty dollars from a planter whose name I can't recall right now, though law would say it is my own as long as I work that plantation, which, I thank the Lord, is that short day and no other.

I'm bought as a stable boy, which is the only truth Jeremiah and I tell in these next years of our shamming and deceiving. Working with horses is the key to my escape plan: With me in the stables, where the visiting buggies park, Jeremiah comes visiting in his buggy-wagon. He claims some kind of business like looking

for an escaped slave or a doctor for some emergency, and once his buggy is parked there, soon as I can move my work in that direction, I stow away in that hiding place in our wagon.

We are two lucky people that first time; two scared-out-of-their-wits people for whom everything goes exactly right. I see Jeremiah arrive near nightfall, I climb into that buggy's secret compartment before anyone knows to pay me any mind, and I just wait to ride out of there with Jeremiah and my most expensive freedom.

Do I believe I'm safe, now? Not for a minute and not for a second. Only when we are far away from that place do I come out from that cramped and suffocating hideaway, purely disbelieving we could have succeeded.

Now Jeremiah hands me the first bills I have ever held in my entire life: half of that nine hundred and fifty dollars. Half a slave's-worth of money. More money than any usual slave will ever see in his life. I stare at those bills because all I see is paper and squiggles and faces—I can't read the numbers to know just what I've got. But on our riding now Jeremiah teaches me something every one of you knows: numbers, those ten simplest of things. So now sometimes our talking is nothing but numbers—the adding and subtracting I do in my head while Jeremiah tells me one number after another. That buggy-wagon is my new schoolroom, I suppose.

So we head on farther north, not saying much to one another. And after weeks and months pass, we do cross the river into Ohio—with problems, every shape and kind of problem, but ones we're able to solve mostly with our lies, our outrunning, our money, and a few gunshots.

This next part is too long to tell so you'll have to take my word that what I'm telling is still true. I've been done with lying for years. Jeremiah's folks find me an older Negro family to live with nearby, and there's work I can do and people like myself who have come north with absolutely nothing but whatever strength they have left. And I do begin working, for nearly all the money has been used up riding and bribing and supplying our way north. But what I want is schooling, and where is a school that will take a Negro like me and start with nothing but the alphabet? I can't even find a school for the Negro children living there, who don't know much more than I do—no, there isn't a school. Slaves who managed their escaping could be free up North, oh yes, but kept just as ignorant as in the South.

And this is how I figure out the next years of my life, doing whatever I do just to build a school where the children done being slaves can learn.

I am a man, I suppose you'd have to say, of almost sixteen now. Picture me just a few months after coming north, walking straight back to the house where Jeremiah's been studying and building chairs alongside his father, and declaring, "There has to be a school built up here for Negro children, and no amount of back-breaking work, which I am willing to do, is going to raise that kind of school-building money. But I believe we could trick some folks out of that building money."

I don't need to say another word; Jeremiah knows what I mean: We could finance that school from the very pockets of the planters themselves, from the very Purgatory of those slave auctions. With all our hearts, we know we're more likely to fail than succeed at the treachery we are about to commit, but we just end up laughing—what else can we discuss? The next morning, Starbright, that same trapdoor buggy, Jeremiah, and your friend Pompey here, we begin our deceiving years together, heading straight south for the nearest auction block. There's only God to guarantee what's ahead—but He must've taken a liking to our school-building idea and blessed us with safety enough to keep us going, trouble enough to keep us watchful and humble.

In Lexington, Kentucky, I put out my hands for Jeremiah to

bind in ropes and he marches my freedom back onto the auction block for the third time in what's still a pretty short life.

That year and the next few I am half-time a free man, and half-time a slave. Neither Jeremiah nor I myself set foot on that Bibb plantation again. I never see my mother, though as I said, I hardly knew her beyond the age of three. New Orleans, Vicksburg, the states of Maryland, Florida, Alabama—I am sold over and over and over again, and, with the grace of God, I find a way to meet up with Jeremiah each time, saving my soul from each of

those devils' plantations. What money my black skin buys us, we divide in half; we don't know then what fate will bring to us in our different lives. We don't exactly have a plan that ends us up here in this city of Madisonville, much less a plan for becoming a strange-enough new family with each other, which we do, or a plan for building that school which this new and beautiful building of yours is sitting on top of right now.

—How many times am I sold, all totaled up? Thirty-nine, unless I've managed to forget a few, which wouldn't be any loss. Most of them lasted a day or two, just long enough to receive my issue of clothing, my work orders, and, sometimes, a driver's welcoming lashings "just to start things out with the proper respect." Between times, Jeremiah and I ride as fast and as far away as we can. Through swamps with mosquitoes that want to suck the life from you. Into forests without a path to guide you. Through shallow streams—bloodhounds lose our scent there. Among mountains without so much as a hut of civilization. By now we're both criminals and maybe even getting known in some parts. Criminals. Those people who paid a high price for Jeremiah's mindful, strong, young stable slave and ended up with no slave at all in no time flat—those men want us caught and punished. But in our hearts, we believe the crime is slavery and the criminals are all people who let it continue eating up and spitting out God's children.

Some places, Jeremiah brings back food from town, but often it's just a meal of paw-paws or persimmons from the road. We are, without a doubt, two always-worried men, but some of that worry-you-can-do-nothing-to-stop turns to laughing, so we laugh at our

cleverness and our trickery, never omitting a thanks to God, of course. Jeremiah and I laugh our nervous way from one auction block to the next, often pursued, and less often caught—we bribe or fight our way free then. Even if there were time this morning, my recollecting mind couldn't tell of all those difficult straits, and that's what's blessed about forgetting, like I said.

For peace of mind, Jeremiah and I sleep sometimes in a hotel. Then I am Mr. Pompey Walker, acting as Jeremiah's manservant. (We had all kinds of clothes, by then, for our disguises.) Or Jeremiah is a holy man of the cloth, and I am a poor African soul this missionary is saving. There are even times when I wear a fake mustache and act the college-student son of a property-owning Negro from the North. There is a bit of fun, I won't deny, in all that disguising and pretending, but we are still acting those parts with our real lives at stake.

Still, most often, I am just the able-bodied, polite stable boy some auctioneer says I am, selling for as much as fourteen hundred, or sometimes for as little as three hundred dollars, when my back is freshly whipped from a slave-driver whose hateful eyes I can't escape from for nearly a month, though Jeremiah Walker invents every variety of excuse to visit that plantation, including the courting of the planter's only (and, if I remember correctly, ugly) daughter.

My throat is dry enough now to signal me I've surely worn out my welcome. How long have I gone on like this? No, don't point to the clock—I know those numbers now, but all's I see is a blur with these old eyes. Mrs. Gilbert, let me end this story with something that is here and now and, as the Lord allows, for always. You have real subjects to teach today.

Years are passed by now, children, and one day, somewhere in Kentucky, Jeremiah Walker says to me, "Do you think there's money enough to end this desperate business of ours?" and he counts what we have and adds that to what we have put into a bank. With that decided, we seek out his parents, ready to burden them with our story much as I have burdened you—but though there is a house remaining, his parents are dead from the same swift death: influenza, which cleared the streets of this town—equal shares of black and white—faster than Noah's flood. Seems a true report of time is full of deaths, and I'm sorry there isn't another truth to tell.

Then and there, not more than a few streets from here, I figure to start saying my good-byes to this man who has stolen me and only me from places that have been killing us Negroes for two hundred years. Jeremiah has his money and whatever friends and relations might comfort him in his new grief. And me, I have my half, and my come-true dream, ready to build this school for what black children find their own conniving or merciful way north.

But no, we do not go our separate ways. Trust me as I report what this man said to me next. It'll help if you think of all the rescuing and running away and fearfulness and struggling together we made of our years. Jeremiah looks straight at me and says, "I am staying here. I'm helping in the building of that school of yours. The two families that meant anything to me are gone. And what family I need is right here: Starbright, who brought us here, and you, Pompey Bibb, standing squarely in front of me."

Yes, I have been calling myself "Walker" all through this retelling, haven't I? But that's out of a life of habit, because I was truly still Pompey Bibb until this very next moment you'll hear of.

So I look at this man, a white man who doesn't own me then any more than I own him (though, as I live and continue to breathe, I know I *owe* only him and God for anything I've come to be thankful for), and I say to Jeremiah, "If you are honestly staying, then let me ask you for one more thing: Give me your name to have as my own name, on account of 'Bibb' is the property of a man in Georgia, and I am as far from there as I am from whatever Africa once bore my mother."

What else is there worth knowing? All that was God-sent in my life, until this day, today, passed by in that minute, when Jeremiah said, "I'm proud to meet you, Pompey Walker," and we shook hands, and then fell against each other, clasping our arms around each other's backs like we meant to squeeze out all the sorry past from each other's lungs. No, I didn't picture what-all I was exhaling forever taking on ghostly shapes like crows and slave-hounding dogs and paddyrollers' horses, but something real and bitter lifted out of my life and never returned.

Jeremiah Walker, and some other needful ex-slaves that we found, and I myself—we did build a school. Sweet Freedom we named it, and it stood for that—stood in this very spot for nearly sixty years, teaching whatever a young child's mind ought to possess, be that child in a white school or a black school. A while after the Civil War, the town gave it another name and a real sign: ELM STREET SCHOOL, but no one who remembered its being built ever called it anything but Sweet Freedom—four rooms at the corner of Elm and Short streets.

And that catches us up to today and right now and this minute where we are all sitting inside this place with many more than four rooms that you're calling after me Pompey Walker Elementary School. Well, I am helpless but to thank you for it, here—me, all by myself, a man who's had enough of retelling.

Please . . . Mrs. Gilbert, don't let them start applauding again. Have them stop. Now, I can't keep you from calling this school what you will, but don't reward anymore this shameless confessing. . . .

So I'll go on and leave you. I've done what I promised, I think—
said everything but enough thanks; there's just no amount that will do.

—Jeremiah Walker? How is it I didn't say? Jeremiah, he passed on
thirty-two years ago—be thirty-three years this coming January the
ninth—taking with him the one true friendship I ever was blessed to
know. Now, please. Mrs. Gilbert, please, dismiss these children and
teach them.

AUTHOR'S NOTE

When Aminah and I finished our first collaboration, *Elijah's Angel,* we began sharing ideas for a new book. Among Aminah's suggestions was another Ohio story that we two native Ohioans might imagine together: the life of Gussie West, a slave who, with a white partner, repeatedly sold himself into slavery and, with the profits, built a school for freed black children.

Visualizing what Aminah might create of this tale inspired me to find a story that could assemble or inhabit the sculptures, paintings, quilts, and scrolls that Aminah had been making, year after year, about slave times. Yet the seed about Gussie West's life—a rather brief news clipping—wouldn't sprout in my imagination. Each draft I began smothered beneath the unbearable weight of slavery: my narrator seemed bound to tell the entire history of the Civil War period, while I wanted to write the story of two men who witness, with their whole lives, one and only one version of that monstrosity so neatly labeled "history."

Eventually I found a voice to retell this story: Pompey Walker's. His is one voice modeled from many, the voices of elderly freed slaves recorded in volumes of recollections. And while Pompey himself is an invention, nearly every event he recounts is true to one or another memoir of that period. The horsehair disguise, the death of the puppies, the whippings, the buggy's hidden compartment—all these actual occurrences entangle in Pompey's voice to create a new life. *A School for Pompey Walker* is not a true story, but it is a real story, one fostered by many lives and united in a voice that, I hope, rings true enough to convince our hearts to feel more than they might from reading an encyclopedia of facts.

This story could be written, then, only because Pompey himself could leave out things that I, as a responsible narrator, could not. He could only recall what happened to him, and even that he could forget at times. Where are the heroic scenes of the Underground Railroad or slave uprisings, the progress of emancipation and Abolition? Far beyond Pompey's speech to the children that one morning. The memories of Aminah's Great-great-aunt Cornelia Johnson, a former slave who died at the age of 105, remain outside Pompey's knowledge. (Thankfully, they are within Aminah's; she has made those recollections of Sapelo Island, Georgia, a vivid, haunting part of this community's life.) Still, Pompey's single character, his storytelling ability, his reluctance to recall, his "saved-up tears," his politeness, and his impatience— all this had to be shared with his audience alongside his life's story.

One last difficulty remained: Pompey's choice of words. In retelling his years, Pompey has to speak a language most natural to a slave in the mid-1800s. Except he must also speak the words of an elderly ex-slave living in the 1920s, remembering to soften them for his audience of school children. But a reader at the end of the twentieth century knows a different spoken language. *Negro, African-American, black,* and certainly the more vicious words that Pompey had heard—each choice dishonors some generation in a story that spans generations.

Finally, I wrote a story about a man whose life I have lived only in my imagination, yet the imagination is often as valuable a teacher as personal experience. Our greatest blessing as human beings is that we can believe in and care for people of every age, color, and origin that we have neither met nor can pretend to be. Understanding those differences reveals the sometimes obscured argument for the kinship that exists among people of all times and all struggles. To tell or to hear a story extends the bonds of humanity rather than the bondage of inhuman ignorance.

Because this is the story of a man's life in and out of slavery, it is necessarily filled with tragedies and agonies. But I hope it can be, as well, a story of a triumphant friendship that manages to confer a sense of family between two individuals that the era would have pitted against one another. I hope it can be a story of courage, even in light of Pompey's humble embarrassment as he stands before the school dedicated in his honor.

In this similar spirit of dedication, Aminah and I gratefully offer this book to every reader who continues to do as Pompey urges at the close of his tale: Teach the children.

—Michael J. Rosen
Columbus, Ohio

Requests for permission to make copies of any part of the work
should be mailed to: Permissions Department,
Harcourt Brace & Company, 6277 Sea Harbor Drive,
Orlando, Florida 32887-6777.

Library of Congress Cataloging-in-Publication Data
Rosen, Michael J., 1954–
A school for Pompey Walker/by Michael J. Rosen; illustrated by
Aminah Brenda Lynn Robinson.—1st ed.
p.   cm.
Summary: At the dedication of a school named after him, an old
former slave tells the story of his life and how, with the help of a
white friend, he managed to save money to build a school for
black children in Ohio by being repeatedly sold into and escaping
from slavery.
ISBN 0-15-200114-X
|1. Slavery—Fiction. 2. Schools—Fiction. 3. Underground
railroad—Fiction. 4. Fugitive slaves—Fiction. 5. Abolitionists—
Fiction. 6. Afro-Americans—Fiction.| I. Robinson, Aminah Brenda
Lynn, ill. II. Title.
PZ7.R71868Sc   1995
|Fic|—dc20   94-6240

First edition
A B C D E

The illustrations in this book were done in colored pencils, inks, and
dyes on 100 percent rag paper.
The display type was set in Las Bonitas.
The text type was set in Granjon by Thompson Type,
San Diego, California.
Color separations by Bright Arts, Ltd., Singapore
Printed and bound by Tien Wah Press, Singapore
This book was printed with soya-based inks on Leykam recycled
paper, which contains more than 20 percent postconsumer waste and
has a total recycled content of at least 50 percent.
Production supervision by Warren Wallerstein and Ginger Boyer
Designed by Lydia D'moch